MR.GRUMBLE

MR. GRUMBLE

by Roger Hargreaves

Mr Grumble's name suited him well!

"Bah!" he would grumble, every morning,
when his alarm clock rang.
"It's the start of yet another
horrible day!"

"Bah!" he would groan every afternoon,
on his walk in the country.
"I hate the countryside!"

One day, just after he said this,
someone suddenly appeared by magic.

It was a wizard.

A wizard, to whom Mr Grumble had the nerve to say, "Bah! I hate wizards who suddenly appear by magic."

"Really?" said the wizard.
"Well, I don't like people who are constantly grumbling and moaning. I'll tell you what I do to people who have bad manners. I turn them into ...

... little pigs!"

And the wizard disappeared,
leaving behind him a very piggy-
looking Mr Grumble.

Mr Grumble was afraid that he might
remain a pig for the rest of his life.

But five minutes later,
by magic, of course,
he changed back into his old self.

He set off again and happened to pass
Little Miss Fun's house.

"Come in!" she cried.
"I'm having a party!"

Mr Grumble went in, but when he heard
Little Miss Fun's guests singing and
laughing he scowled.

"Bah!" he moaned.
"I can't stand singing and laughing!"

He would have done better to
have kept quiet, because ...

... the wizard appeared once more.

"I see that my first lesson
wasn't enough!" he said.
"If I'm going to teach you to stop grumbling,
groaning and moaning, I'll have to do
more than turn you into a little pig,
I'll have to turn you into ...

... a big pig!"

Mr Grumble did not like it one bit.

Little Miss Fun and her guests, however, found it very funny.

"Please," begged Mr Grumble,
"turn me back to normal!
I promise that I will never grumble,
groan or moan ever again!"

And he feebly wiggled his curly tail.

The wizard took pity on him,
and changed him back into his old self.

And then the wizard disappeared again.

Then Little Miss Fun jumped onto a table and pretended to be a clown.

Mr Grumble was not amused.

"Bah!" he snorted.
"I can't stand people who jump onto tables and pretend to be clowns!"

You can guess what happened next.

He turned into ...

... an enormous pig!

An enormous pig whose face was
red with embarrassment!

"Oink!" wailed Mr Grumble, mournfully.

Then, this enormous red-faced pig,
made a solemn promise.

"Never again will I grumble, groan,
moan or snort!"

"Good," said the wizard,
suddenly appearing once again.

And Mr Grumble changed back
into his old self.

Well, not exactly his old self!

Look at that nice smile on his face.

Amazing, isn't it?

Later, Mr Grumble went home.

And, tired out after his exhausting day,
he went straight to bed.

He slept the whole night
without once grumbling,
groaning, moaning or snorting.

But not without ...

... snoring!

Fantastic offers for Mr. Men fans!

Collect all your Mr. Men or Little Miss books in these superb durable collectors' cases!
Only £5.99 inc. postage and packing, these wipe-clean, hard-wearing cases will give all your Mr. Men or Little Miss books a beautiful new home!

Keep track of your collection with this giant-sized double-sided Mr. Men and Little Miss Collectors' poster.
Collect 6 tokens and we will send you a brilliant giant-sized double-sided collectors' poster! Simply tape a £1 coin to cover postage and packaging in the space provided and fill out the form overleaf.

STICK £1 COIN HERE
(for poster only)

Only need a few Mr. Men or Little Miss to complete your set? You can order any of the titles on the back of the books from our Mr. Men order line on 0870 787 1724. Orders should be delivered between 5 and 7 working days.

─── **TO BE COMPLETED BY AN ADULT** ───

To apply for any of these great offers, ask an adult to complete the details below and send this whole page with the appropriate payment and tokens, to: MR. MEN CLASSIC OFFER, PO BOX 715, HORSHAM RH12 5WG

☐ Please send me a giant-sized double-sided collectors' poster.
AND ☐ I enclose 6 tokens and have taped a £1 coin to the other side of this page.

☐ Please send me ☐ Mr. Men Library case(s) and/or ☐ Little Miss library case(s) at £5.99 each inc P&P

☐ I enclose a cheque/postal order payable to Egmont UK Limited for £..........................

OR ☐ Please debit my MasterCard / Visa / Maestro / Delta account (delete as appropriate) for £..........................

Card no. ☐☐☐☐ ☐☐☐☐ ☐☐☐☐ ☐☐☐☐ ☐☐☐☐   Security code ☐☐☐

Issue no. (if available) ☐☐   Start Date ☐☐/☐☐/☐☐   Expiry Date ☐☐/☐☐/☐☐

Fan's name: ....   Date of birth: ....

Address: ....

....

Postcode: ....

Name of parent / guardian: ....

Email for parent / guardian: ....

Signature of parent / guardian: ....

Please allow 28 days for delivery. Offer is only available while stocks last. We reserve the right to change the terms of this offer at any time and we offer a 14 day money back guarantee. This does not affect your statutory rights. Offers apply to UK only.

☐ We may occasionally wish to send you information about other Egmont children's books.
If you would rather we didn't, please tick this box.

Ref: MRM 001